LEO COCKROACH... TOY TESTER

KEVIN O'MALLEY

Walker and Company ✺ New York

This is Leo, Leo Cockroach.

The lady with the shoe is Mildred Splatt, president and CEO of Waddatoy Toys.

Leo lives in Ms. Splatt's desk. And though she doesn't know it, Leo works at the toy company, too.

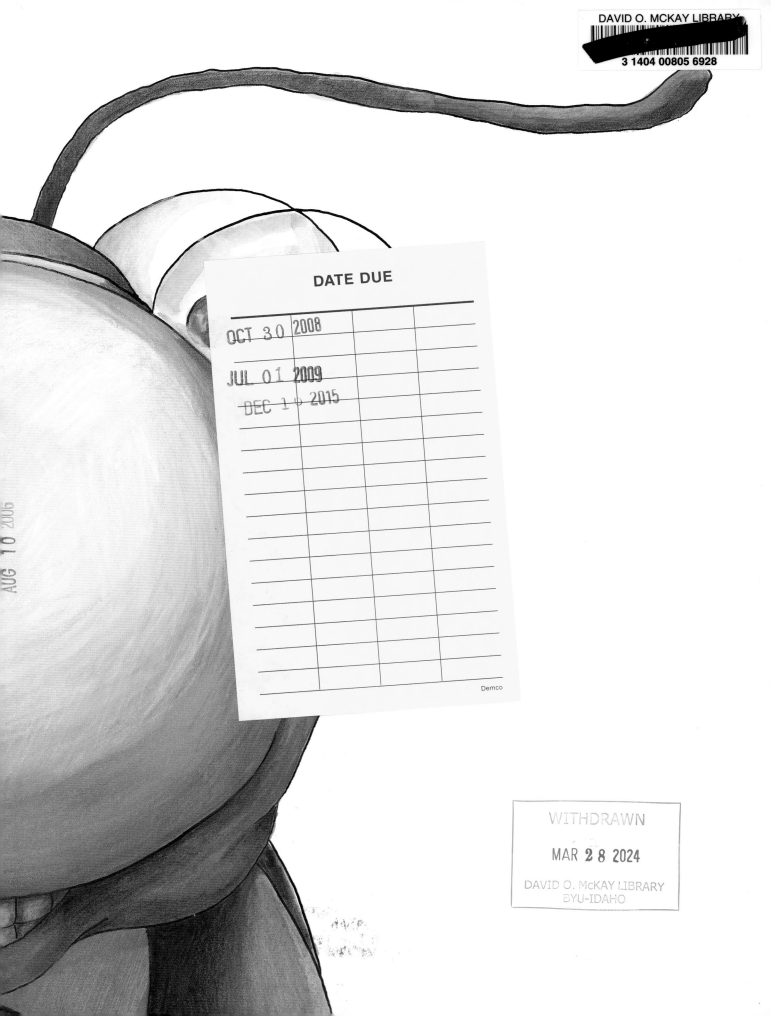

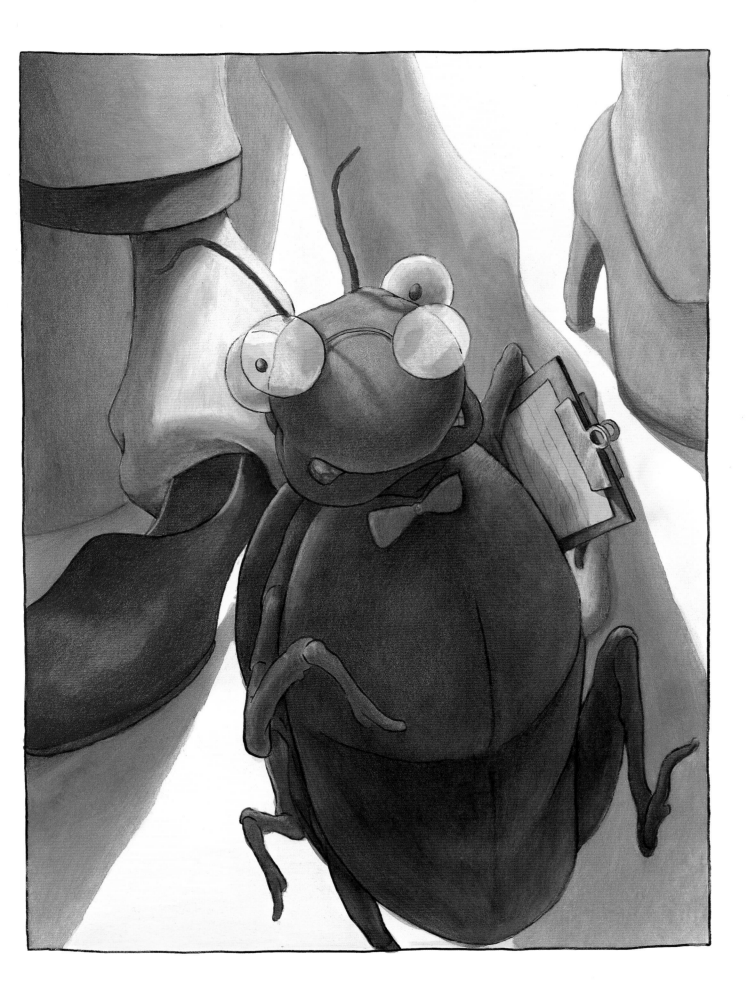

Leo is a toy tester.

He works at night. And he's good at his job.

Testing toys is hard work, and it can be downright dangerous for a cockroach.

When Leo finds a winner,
he takes it back to Ms. Splatt's office
with the help of his only real friend,
a cat named Bernard.

It hadn't taken long for Mildred Splatt
to realize that these little gems would fly off the
shelves of the toy store. And she had come to
rely on these nocturnal surprises to keep her
company in business.

Leo didn't mind so much that Mildred took all the credit;
he enjoyed his work.

The problem was that Ms. Mildred Splatt hated cockroaches.
She thought Leo was a disgusting little pest.

Everytime she spotted him,
Mildred tried to **squash** him.

"Bernard," Leo panted, "that lady really bugs me."

Bernard just sighed.

"Cockroaches might be spineless,
but tonight I'm getting a backbone.
I'm going to fly that plane right over
to the toy company across the street.
Let's see who brings Mildred toys *then*."

That night, the two friends hugged each other before Leo scurried aboard the plane.

"Bernard, my good friend, look for me across the street. Life is bound to be better there."

"You could try writing Ms. Splatt a letter," said Bernard.

"Too late for that," yelled Leo as the plane flew out the window.

At first Leo's flying abilities left something to be desired.
But after a few minor corrections, he was flying like a fly.

Soon he would be landing in the office of Mr. Magnus Worm,
president and CEO of Notsogouda Toys.

Landing might be too soft a word.

Crashing is more like it.

When he came to, Leo found himself in a furnished cage, front and center on the desk of the boss himself.

"**Well, well,** well," thought Leo, "this isn't half bad."

Mr. Worm seemed a pleasant enough fellow when he strode through the door.

After introducing himself, Leo described how he had gotten to Mr. Worm's office.

"Now," said Leo, "if you will open the door of my beautiful new home, I will begin testing your fine toys."

"I think it would be better if we brought the toys to you," Magnus Worm replied.

"How marvelous," thought Leo. "Finally I'm getting the respect I deserve."

Toys of all shapes and sizes were brought before him. And on every occasion Leo was forced to tell Mr. Worm that his toys were junk. Not just unpleasant to play with but unsafe as well!

Mr. Magnus Worm was earwigging out.

Leo started to think that maybe he'd made a mistake.

He really missed Bernard. And he wasn't even allowed out of his cage anymore.

All he could do was look out through the bars and rate the new toys—thumbs-up for good, thumbs-down for bad.

Unfortunately, Leo could never give anything the thumbs-up.

Mr. Magnus Worm was as angry as a swarm of bees.

Things were looking bad for Leo. Worse, in a way, than when he worked for Mildred Splatt.

Leo thought, "If I could just get out of this cage, I'd head back across the street. Better to run from a shoe than to live like a slave."

As luck would have it, Mr. Worm placed a rocket on his desk for Leo's judgment.

It was poorly made and badly painted, but it was Leo's only chance.

Winging it, Leo made up a story about having to test-fly the rocket before he could rate it.

Surprisingly, Magnus Worm agreed.

At first, the rocket dipped, swooped, and flew upside down.

Finally, Leo managed to point it in the direction of the window.

Ramming the throttle forward, the rocket raced through the window and into the blue sky.

Halfway across the street, the engine stopped.

Leo thought he was headed for the big roach motel in the sky.

Pointing the nose of the rocket toward Mildred's window, Leo crossed all his legs and said a prayer.

When he opened his eyes, the first thing he saw
was his friend, Bernard. Such joy, such happiness!

Leo told Bernard about his life at Notsogouda Toys, and Bernard
told Leo about how Mildred Splatt hadn't had a hit toy since Leo had
left. She was bugging out.

"Well, then," said Leo, "I had best get my legs in gear.
But I'm telling you right now, my good cat, it's not going to be like it
was before. No more trying to stomp me or poison me or anything.
I'm taking your advice. I'm going to write Mildred a letter."

And things worked out for Leo, even better than he expected.

FOR MELISSA, HARRY, IAN, AND THEIR NEW BABY, EVAN. AND IN MEMORY OF OUR AUNT MILDRED.

First published in the United States of America in 1999 by Walker Publishing Company, Inc.

Published simultaneously in Canada by Thomas Allen & Son Canada, Limited, Markham, Ontario

Library of Congress Cataloging-in-Publication Data
O'Malley, Kevin.
Leo Cockroach . . . toy tester/Kevin O'Malley.
p.   cm.
Summary: Leo Cockroach, who secretly tests toys for the bug-hating president of a toy company, seeks a job with the competitor across the street and finds himself worse off than before.
ISBN 0-8027-8689-8H. —ISBN 0-8027-8690-1R
[1. Cockroaches—Fiction. 2. Toys—Fiction.] I. Title.
PZ7.0526Le   1999
[E]—dc21   98-27989
                                            CIP
                                            AC

Book design by Sophie Ye Chin

Printed in Hong Kong

10 9 8 7 6 5 4 3 2 1

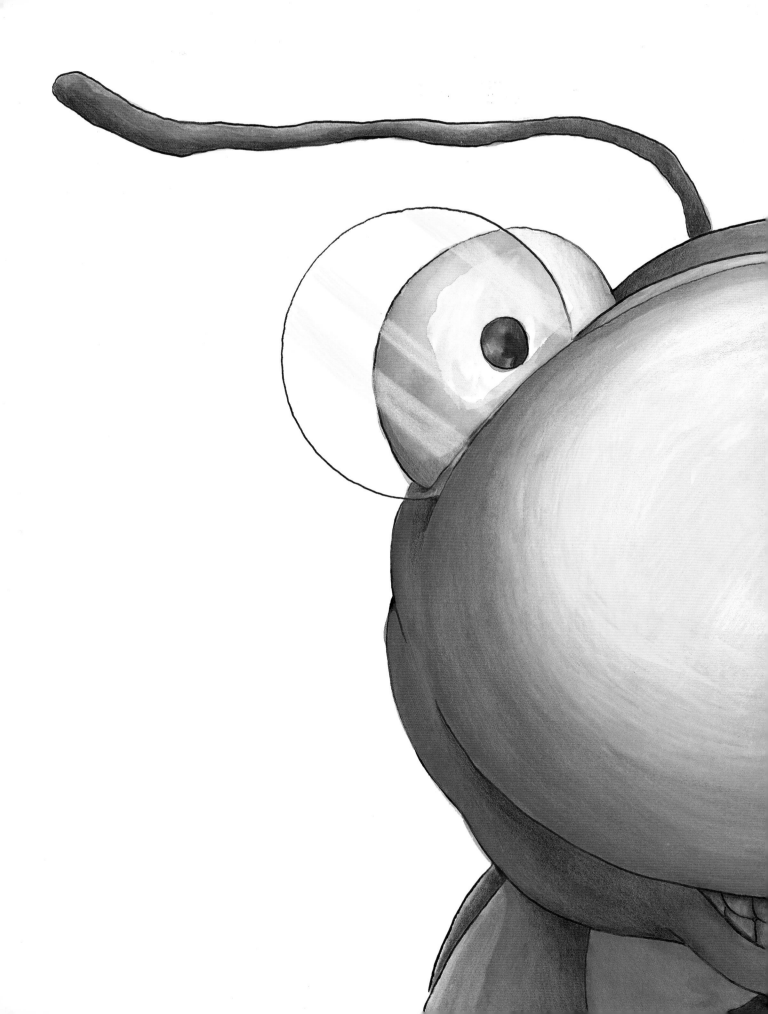